JAMES

PERCY

MEET ALL THESE FRIENDS IN BUZZ BOOKS:

Thomas the Tank Engine
Fireman Sam
Bugs Bunny
Toucan 'Tecs
Barney
Police Academy
Looney Tunes
Flintstones
Jetsons

First published 1992 by Buzz Books,
an imprint of Reed International Books Ltd
Michelin House, 81 Fulham Road, London SW3 6RB

LONDON MELBOURNE AUCKLAND

ISBN 1 85591 211 2

Printed and bound in Great Britain by BPCC Hazell Books,
Paulton and Aylesbury

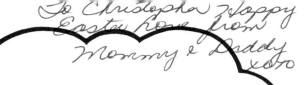

PERCY TAKES THE PLUNGE

buzz books

One day Henry puffed wearily into the station. He wanted to rest in the shed but Percy was talking to Bill and Ben, the twin tank engines. He was telling them about the time he had braved bad weather to help Thomas.

". . . It was raining hard. Water swirled
under my boiler," said Percy dramatically.
"I couldn't see where I was going, but I
struggled on . . ."

"Oooh, Percy, you *are* brave," said Bill.

"Well, it wasn't anything really," smiled Percy. "Water's nothing to an engine with determination."

"Tell us more, Percy," said Ben.

"What are *you* engines doing here?" hissed Henry, suddenly. "This shed is for the Fat Controller's engines. Go away!"

"Silly things," Henry snorted as Bill and Ben ran off.

"They're not silly," said Percy. He had been enjoying himself and was cross because Henry had sent them away.

"They are silly, and so are you,"
muttered Henry. " 'Water's nothing to an
engine with determination.' Huh!"

"Anyway," said cheeky Percy. "I'm not
afraid of water. I like it."

Percy ran off to the harbour, singing,

*"Once an engine attached to a train
was afraid of a few drops of rain."*

"No one ever lets me forget the time I wouldn't come out of the tunnel in case the rain spoilt my paint," huffed Henry.

When Percy reached the harbour he found Thomas on the quay. Thomas was looking at an old board. It read: DANGER! ENGINES MUST NOT PASS THIS BOARD.

"We mustn't go past it," Thomas said. "That's orders."

"Why?" asked Percy.

" 'DANGER' means falling down something," replied Thomas wisely. "I went past 'DANGER' once," he said, "and fell down a mine."

Percy looked beyond the board. "I can't see a mine," he said. He didn't know that the foundations of the quay had sunk and that the rails now sloped downward to the sea.

"Stupid board!" said Percy, crossly.

For days and days afterwards he tried to sidle past it, but his driver stopped him every time.

Then Percy made a plan.

One day, as he made his way to the harbour, he whispered to the trucks, "Will you give me a bump when we get to the quay?"

The trucks were surprised. They had never been asked to bump an engine before. They giggled and chattered about it all the way through the journey.

"The driver doesn't know my plan," chuckled Percy.

"On! On! On!" laughed the trucks. Percy thought that they were helping.

"I'll pretend to stop at the station, but the trucks will push me past the board," he said. "Then I'll make them stop. I can do that whenever I like."

If Percy hadn't been so conceited, he
would never have been so silly. Every wise
engine knows that you cannot trust trucks.

They reached the quay and Percy's
brakes groaned. *That* was the signal for the
trucks.

"Go on! Go on!" they yelled and bumped
Percy's driver and fireman off the footplate.

"Ow!" said Percy, sliding past the board.
The rails were slippery. His wheels wouldn't
grip.

Percy was frantic. "That's enough!" he hissed. But it was too late. Once on the slope, he slithered down into the sea.

Percy was sunk.

"You are a very disobedient engine."
Percy knew that voice. He groaned.

"Please sir," said Percy. "Get me out, sir.
I'm truly sorry, sir."

"No, Percy," said the Fat Controller. "We cannot do that till high tide. I hope this will teach you to obey orders."

''Yes, sir,'' Percy shivered. He was cold.
Fish were playing hide and seek through his
wheels. The tide rose higher and higher.

It was dark when the men brought floating cranes to rescue Percy.

Percy was too cold and stiff to move by himself, so the next day he was sent to the works on Henry's goods train.

"Well, well, well!" chuckled Henry. "Did you like the water?"

"No!" muttered Percy.

"I *am* surprised," smiled Henry. "You
need more determination, Percy. 'Water's
nothing to an engine with determination,'
you know. Perhaps you would like it better
next time."

But Percy is quite determined that there won't be a "next time"!

THOMAS

EDWARD

GORDON